IN THE DARK CAVE

By

Richard Watson

Illustrated by

Dean Norman

STAR BRIGHT BOOKS

NEW YORK

Deep in the dark cave
lived the cave cricket,
where water came down
like out of a spigot.

Back in the passage
lived the cave rat.

Over his head
hung down the cave bat.

In the depths of the cave
it was always night.

But none of these creatures
needed a light.

The crafty cave cricket
had feelers <u>this</u> long.

The brown cave bat
sang a sweet song.

The cave cricket crept
by feeling the walls.

The cave bat flew
through echoing halls.

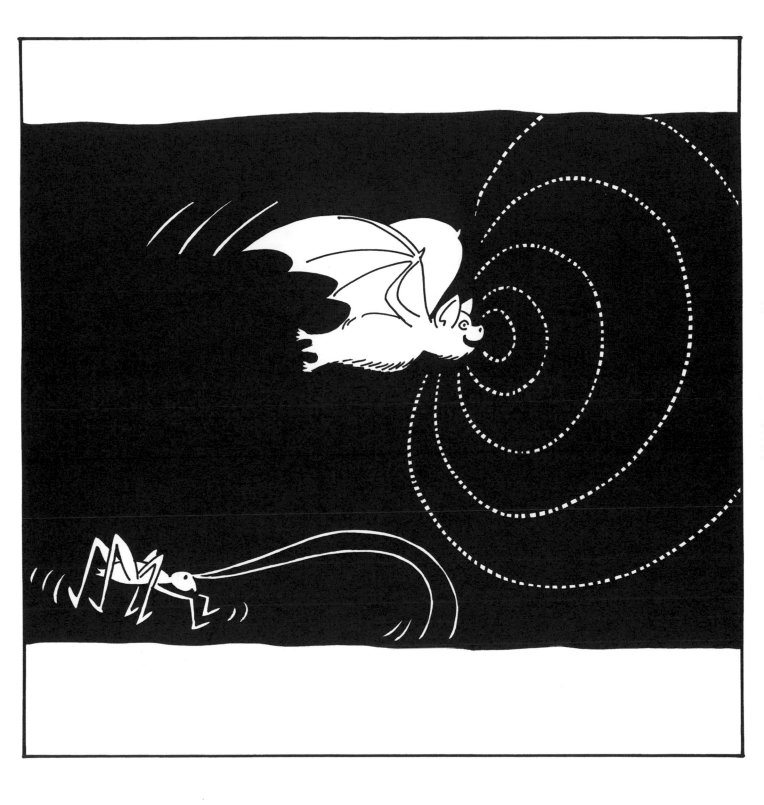

The bold cave rat
got about quite well.

He knew what's where
by the way things smell.

They lived together
in that deep dark place,
far from people
in the earth's embrace.

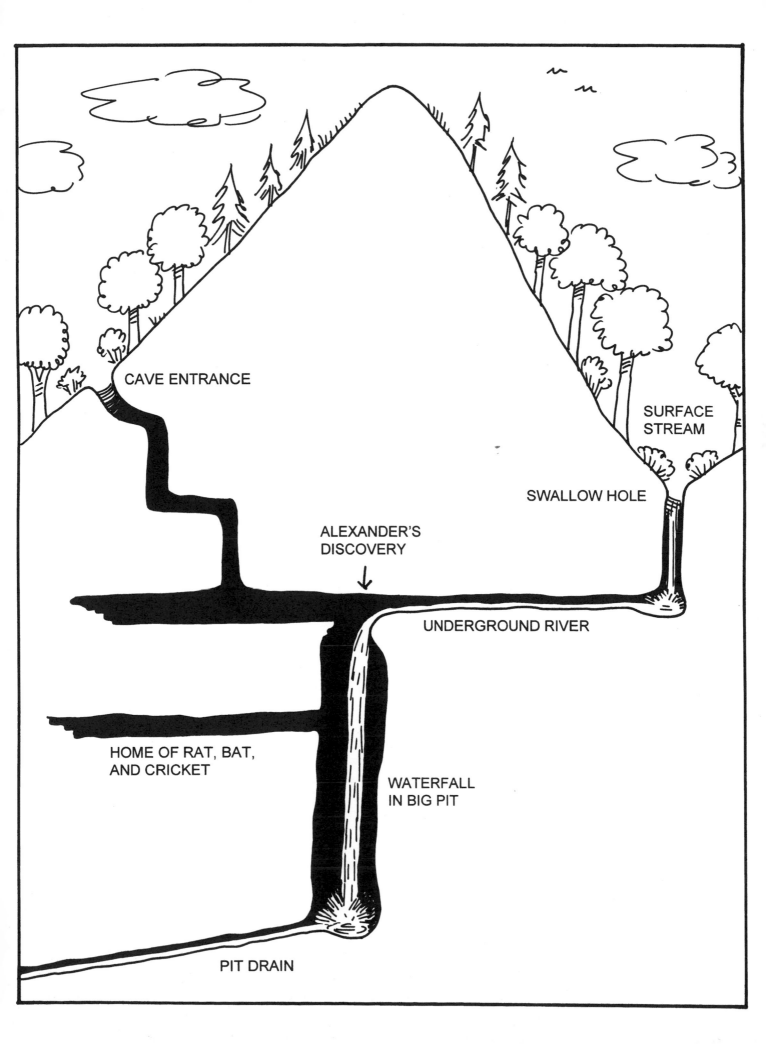

CAVE ENTRANCE

SURFACE STREAM

SWALLOW HOLE

ALEXANDER'S DISCOVERY

UNDERGROUND RIVER

HOME OF RAT, BAT, AND CRICKET

WATERFALL IN BIG PIT

PIT DRAIN

Deep in that darkness
it was impossible to see.

They thought that was always
the way it would be.

Then suddenly appeared,
in the shaft up high,
a pinpoint of light,
like a star in the sky.

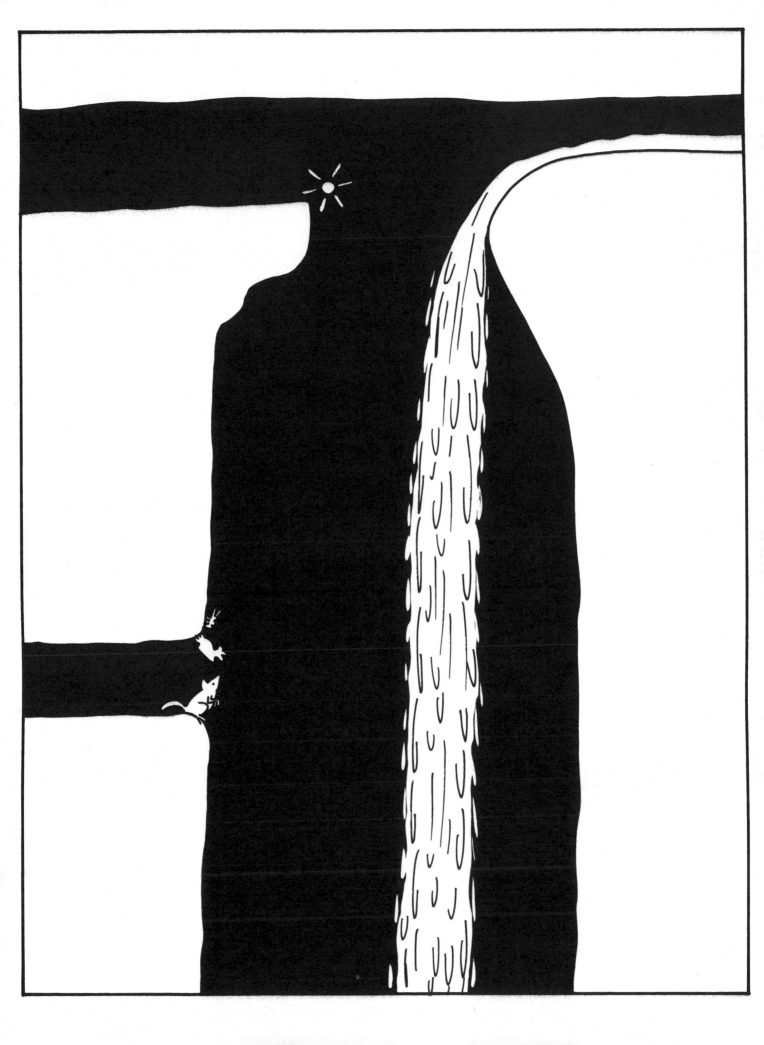

Down the great pit
came a thin line of rope.

And down the line slowly, came
Alexander James Augustus Pope.

On his head was a helmet,
on the helmet a lamp.

And from it shown down
a light through the damp.

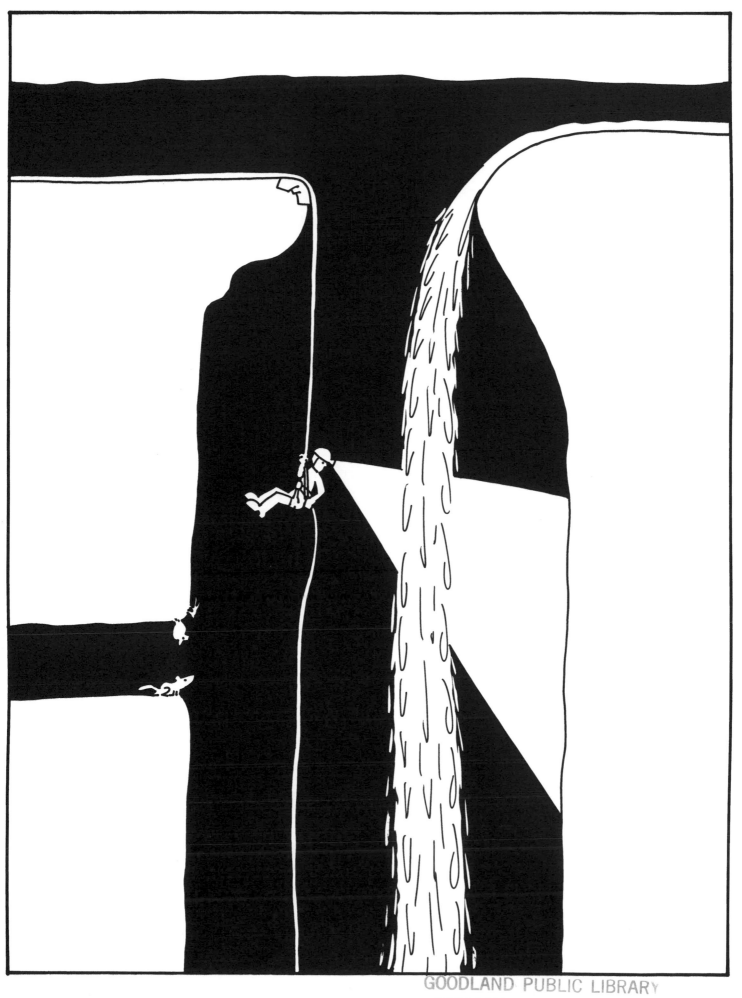

Alexander was exploring the dark underground.

This was the deepest cave he had found.

The cricket, the bat,
and the bold cave rat
stared in wonder
at the light on the hat.

Alexander slid
to the depths below.

The three cave creatures
watched him go.

Soon he shouted,
"It bottoms out!"

And he climbed back up
past the water spout.

The light faded
as he went away.

That was the end
of the <u>only</u> day.

For a long time after
the creatures just sat—
the cricket, the bat, and
the bold cave rat.

It was unbelievable,
like in a dream.

They almost forgot
what they had seen.

But sometimes now
in the depths below,
they seem to see
the darkness glow.

Deep in the dark cave
lives the bat.

So does the cricket
and the bold cave rat.

Published in the United States of America by Star Bright Books, Inc., New York. The name Star Bright Books and the Star Bright Books logo are registered trademarks of Star Bright Books, Inc. Please visit www.starbrightbooks.com.

ISBN-13: 978-1-59572-038-2
ISBN-10: 1-59575-038-3

Printed in China 9 8 7 6 5 4 3 2 1

Library of Congress Cataloging-in-Publication Data

Watson, Richard A., 1931-
  In the dark cave / by Richard Watson ; illustrated by Dean Norman.
      p. cm.
  Summary: A cave cricket, a cave rat, and a bat live contentedly in the dark until suddenly one day an explorer appears, bringing with him a beam of light.
  ISBN-13: 978-1-59572-038-2
  ISBN-10: 1-59572-038-3
 [1. Cave animals--Fiction. 2. Caves--Fiction. 3. Stories in rhyme.] I. Norman, Dean, ill. II. Title.

PZ8.3.W3436Inat 2005
[E]--dc22
                                              2005012908